ADVENTURES
AT
HOUND HOTEL

PICTURE WINDOW BOOKS
A Capstone Imprint

Adventures at Hound Hotel is published by Picture Window Books
A Capstone Imprint
1710 Roe Crest Drive
North Mankato, Minnesota 56003
www.capstonepub.com

Library of Congress Cataloging-in-Publication Data
Sateren, Shelley Swanson, author.
Growling Gracie/by Shelley Sateren; illustrated by Deborah Melmon.
pages cm. — (Adventures at Hound Hotel)
Summary: When they are not fighting with each other Alfie Wolfe and his twin
sister Alfreeda help out with their mother's dog hotel business — but just
now he is faced with a friendly pug called Twinkles, and an aggressive Golden
Retriever, named Gracie, who seems to regard him as a threat.
ISBN 978-1-4795-5899-5 (library binding)
ISBN 978-1-4795-5903-9 (paperback.)
ISBN 978-1-4795-6193-3 (ebook)

1. Golden retriever—Juvenile fiction. 2. Pug—Juvenile fiction. 3. Dogs—Juvenile
fiction. 4. Kennels—Juvenile fiction. 5. Twins—Juvenile fiction. 6. Brothers and
sisters—Juvenile fiction. [1. Golden retriever—Fiction. 2. Pug—Fiction. 3. Dogs—
Fiction. 4. Kennels—Fiction. 5. Twins—Fiction. 6. Brothers and sisters--Fiction.] I.
Melmon, Deborah, illustrator. II. Title.
PZ7.S249155Gr 2015
813.54—dc23   2014023821

Designer: Russell Griesmer

Printed in China.
092014   008473RRDS15

Growling Gracie

by Shelley Swanson Sateren

illustrated by Deborah Melmon

TABLE OF CONTENTS

CHAPTER 1
Purple in the Face 9

CHAPTER 2
Spot Gets Fighting Mad 18

CHAPTER 3
Whoa There, Bud 27

CHAPTER 4
Tug of Beak 36

CHAPTER 5
Rooster Soup and Roasted Kid 42

CHAPTER 6
This Is MY Territory, Dude 50

CHAPTER 7
It's Your Fault, Alfie 57

CHAPTER 8
Frisbee Land! 64

ADVENTURES AT HOUND HOTEL

IT'S TIME FOR YOUR ADVENTURE AT HOUND HOTEL!

At Hound Hotel, dogs are given the royal treatment. We are a top-notch boarding kennel. When your dog stays with us, we will follow your feeding schedule, give them walks, and tuck them in at night.

We are always just a short walk away from the dogs — the kennels are located in a heated building at the end of our driveway. Every dog has his or her own pen, with a bed, blanket, and water dish.

Rest assured . . . a stay at the Hound Hotel is like a vacation for your dog. We have a large play yard, plenty of toys, and pool time in the summer. Your dog will love playing with the other guests.

HOUND HOTEL
WHO'S WHO

WINIFRED WOLFE
Hound Hotel is run by Winifred Wolfe, a lifelong dog lover. Winifred loves dogs of all sorts. She wants to spend time with every breed. When she's not taking care of the canines, she writes books about — you guessed it — dogs.

ALFIE AND ALFREEDA WOLFE
Winifred's young twins help out as much as they can. Whether your dog needs gentle attention or extra playtime, Alfreeda and Alfie provide special services you can't find anywhere else. Your dog will never get bored with these two on the job.

WOLFGANG WOLFE
Winifred's husband pitches in at the hotel whenever he can, but he spends much of his time traveling to study wolf packs. Wolfgang is a real wolf lover — he even named his children after pack leaders, the alpha wolves. Every wolf pack has two alpha wolves: a male one and a female one, just like the Wolfe family twins.

Next time your family goes on vacation, bring your dog to Hound Hotel.

Your pooch is sure to have a howling good time!

CHAPTER 1
Purple in the Face

I'm Alfie Wolfe, and I'm here to tell you all about Gracie the fighting machine. I mean, Gracie the golden retriever.

Sure, she acts nice, calm, and quiet when you first meet her. But watch your back. If you turn on her, she'll turn on you! She'll bark and snarl and leap at you teeth-first. She might even draw blood if you're not careful!

Gracie reminds me of my sister. Sometimes Alfreeda acts like Top Fight Picker of the World!

She gets super crabby when she's tired or sick or hungry. Then it doesn't matter what I do, it bugs her. If I don't do everything totally right, she chews my head off.

(Okay, I admit: I get crabby too sometimes. Mostly when I don't get to play enough with the dogs or with my friends.)

Anyhow, this story isn't about my sister. Well, not totally. It's about Gracie — and her little sister, Twinkles the pug.

Their human mom, Doris, calls them her "baby girls." So we call them sisters.

I first met Gracie and Twinkles last year. Last July to be exact. A crazy-busy weekend at our dog hotel to be exacter.

Our uncle, Robert, brought them over that Saturday morning. See, the dog's owner, Doris, was Uncle Robert's new girlfriend. We hadn't even met Doris yet.

The kennels were booked solid that weekend. Mom, Alfreeda, and I had been working like dogs for two days straight. Our workdays were super long. They started before Spot, our rooster, even crowed. Then we worked until midnight!

My dad couldn't help in the kennels. He was Up North again, studying wolves in the wilderness.

Normally, running a dog hotel meant lots of fun. But we were so busy, that there was just tons of work, taking care of those dogs. I couldn't wait to have some actual *fun* with them.

At about nine o'clock that Saturday morning, we were knocking through a long list of chores. Alfreeda was sitting on the floor inside pen seven.

"Hurry up!" she snapped at me then yawned real wide. Her droopy eyes were half closed.

I yawned right back at her and headed into pen seven. I tossed a little dog bed onto the floor.

"What took you so long?" she demanded.

I was too tired to fight back. I just yawned again and kind of teetered from side to side.

But Alfreeda wouldn't let up. "How come

it took you ten minutes to get one teensy dog bed from the storeroom, huh?" she growled at me.

"It wasn't ten minutes!" I said.

"Was too!" she snapped. "At this rate, we'll get the morning chores done by next month!"

Her face was turning kind of purple. The veins stuck out on her neck.

Well, I sure wasn't going to let Alfreeda be the only alpha fighter around our place. (In case you don't know, "alpha" means "first" or "top." In wolf packs, the alpha male and the alpha female are the biggest, smartest, bravest, strongest, and fastest wolves. And yeah, they're the most fierce too. They take care of the weaker ones.)

I frowned hard at my sister and yelled, "Stop yelling at me! Mom, Alfreeda won't quit yelling at me!"

"*Shh*," Mom said in a super-firm voice. She frowned at us through the chain-link fence. She sat on the floor of pen eight and rocked a homesick dog in her arms. "No fighting today, you two! And I mean it!"

Whoa. I couldn't remember the last time Mom had sounded that crabby.

She went on in that crabby voice, "I got about three hours of sleep last night, thanks to four homesick dogs. I won't stand for a second of your fighting this morning!"

That shut us right up.

About then, Uncle Robert's super-loud car came roaring up outside. His old sports car made the loudest bangs and backfires you've ever heard. You could hear him coming from a mile away.

"Oh, no," Mom said with a groan. "I already told him — not today!"

Okay, so that was weird. Mom always liked it when her brother hung around the hotel. Sometimes he even helped out.

Mom and Uncle Robert fought like cats and dogs when they were kids. But now they're good friends. I'm telling you, that will never happen to my sister and me. Not in a hundred years.

The backfires got real loud, which meant his car was right outside the kennel building. "Uncle Robert's here!" Alfreeda and I yelled at the same time.

We jumped up and bolted for the pen door. We loved Uncle Robert! He gave us gum and stuff. And he always swung us around super fast. It was better than any fair ride!

The race was on for the first swing! Alfreeda and I shoved each other, good and hard, in the pen doorway. We were both trying to blast through first. I won't say who won the shoving match. (Because she always wins. I hate that!)

Alfreeda tore down the hall and through the office. I tore after her. She threw open the front door and yelled, "Swing me first, Uncle Robert!"

"No, me!" I yelled.

"Hey, are those Doris's dogs, Uncle Robert?" Alfreeda called and leaped off the front steps.

She ran toward the car. Two dogs hung out the windows, sniffing all the cool country smells.

Uncle Robert leaned against his car and

grinned at Alfreeda. "Yeah," he said. "Meet Gracie and Twinkles. Twinkles is the best disk dog I've ever met. Throw a Frisbee high, throw it far — she catches it every time."

"Cool!" I said and ran toward them. "I call Twinkles!"

"No way!" Alfreeda yelled. "Whoever touches Twinkles first gets to play Frisbee with her first!"

And then she plopped her hand right on top of the little pug's head.

❧— CHAPTER 2 —❧
Spot Gets Fighting Mad

About one second later, Alfreeda had both dogs out of the car. They already had their leashes on.

I leaped over and yanked the leashes right out of her hand.

"Give them back, Alfie!" she said.

Then the dogs yanked the leashes right out of my hand. Alfreeda shouldn't have yelled like that! It's all her fault that the dogs bolted.

They tore up our long driveway, all the way

18

to our house. Then they ran around the house, past the garden, and through the apple trees.

Gracie was in the lead. Twinkles was a close second.

The leashes came in third, flying behind the dogs.

Gracie and Twinkles tore across the farmyard and started to run around the chicken coop. They tore around it a bunch of times, so fast they were almost a blur.

Spot, our rooster, went crazy. So did the chickens. They flapped their wings and squawked like mad. I'm telling you, feathers rained in the farmyard!

Gracie and Twinkles wouldn't stop bugging the hens, and Spot got fighting mad. He sprang at Twinkles and tried to peck her nose. He missed and tried again.

"Look out, Twinkles!" I shouted. "That rooster's as big as you are. He could really hurt you. Get away!"

"Don't just stand there yelling, Alfie," Alfreeda said and rolled her eyes. "Do something!"

But she beat me to it. She dashed right over and grabbed Twinkles away from Spot.

Alfreeda darted to a tree, not too far from the chicken coop. She dug in her pocket and pulled out a handful of little bone-shaped doggie treats for Twinkles.

Twinkles didn't even wiggle in her arms. She didn't try to get down or anything. Of course not . . . not when somebody gives you ten doggie treats instead of one!

"Hey!" I yelled. "Mom says no more than one treat to hotel guests. Stop trying to win Twinkles away from me!"

"Gracie and Twinkles aren't guests!" Alfreeda yelled back. "They're not paying. They're not staying overnight. They're just visitors!"

She had a point. Anyhow, I didn't even have a chance to yell something back. That second, Gracie sprang at Spot and took a fierce snap at him.

Whoa! Gracie almost had rooster pie for her morning snack!

Uncle Robert hollered, "Gracie, come!" He put his fingers in his mouth and whistled.

But Gracie got even fiercer with Spot. She nipped at his skinny yellow legs and then at his flapping brown feathers. To be honest, I'm not crazy about crabby old Spot. But I didn't want him dead.

I clapped my hands and yelled, "Gracie, come!"

But she wouldn't quit!

Then Alfreeda marched right up to Gracie, with Twinkles still in her arms. She leaned in so close that Twinkles got a little slap from Spot's wing.

"Stop, Gracie," Alfreeda said. "Come."

Well, I couldn't believe my eyeballs. Gracie backed away from Spot and stood beside Alfreeda. Spot backed off too.

Gracie panted hard and stared at my sister, waiting for her next command.

Alfreeda took Gracie's leash and led her to Uncle Robert. Gracie didn't try to break free or anything.

Alfreeda handed the leash to Uncle Robert. She dug in her pocket and gave Gracie a whole handful of dog treats, too. Like about twenty!

That's when I noticed: Alfreeda's jeans pockets were stuffed with dog treats. She must have smelled like a doggie-treat factory. Of course Gracie and Twinkles were following her around without a fight.

"Wow!" Uncle Robert did a long, slow whistle. He gave Alfreeda a high five. "No question, kid! Whenever Doris is gone, you're her dogs' new pack leader!"

I thought, *What? Can't he see that her pockets are jammed with dog snacks? It's just a trick!*

I was so annoyed, I couldn't even talk.

Alfreeda said thank you and bowed. She popped right back up and took another bow.

Suddenly I was fighting mad. "Hey!" I yelled at her.

She looked at me. "What, Alfie?" she asked in her tired-teacher voice.

"Give me Twinkles," I demanded.

"No," she said. "I'm taking her to the play yard. We're going to play a killer game of Frisbee —"

"Oh, no you're not," Mom interrupted her.

We all spun around. Mom stood on the front steps of the kennel building. Her hands were on her hips.

"Robert," she said in a firm voice. "Take those dogs back to Doris's apartment. Now."

"Ah, come on, sis, let them stay," Uncle Robert begged. "I can't take care of Gracie for a whole day. She hates me! She's going to draw blood one of these times!"

"Don't be silly," Mom said. "I'm sure Gracie's a perfectly gentle dog most of the time. We're just too busy to take on another dog, much less two."

Well, I couldn't just stand there and watch the best disk dog in the world take off. I had to play Frisbee with Twinkles! I dashed across the driveway, leaped onto the steps, and grabbed Mom's hands.

I wrapped her fingers nice and tight in mine. Then I held them nice and sweet against my heart.

"Mommy?" I said, just like I used to when I was a little kid. That always used to make Mom give in when I wanted something. I'd just say "Mommy" instead of "Mom."

"Please, Mommy," I begged. "Let Twinkles stay. I've been working and working. Can't I play Frisbee with her, just for five little minutes? Oh *pleeeease*, Mommy?"

Mom stared at me.

I was all set for a big grin and a *yes*.

CHAPTER 3
Whoa There, Bud

That's when Mom totally lost her cool.

She dropped my hands and cried, "I don't have time for this! I'm *sooo* busy! And I'm *sooo* tired!"

She marched around me and down the steps. She headed straight for Uncle Robert.

Mom stopped right in front of him and put her nose up to his. "N. O." You know Mom is serious when she spells her answers.

"Please, Winifred?" he begged. "*You* don't

have to hang out with Twinkles or the monster, I mean, Gracie. Let the twins!"

"Robert!" Mom cried. "You don't get it! They can't hang out with Doris's dogs because I need their help! Eleven dogs need walks, water, baths, brushing, feeding, and comforting! Maybe the kids can play after dinner, but they cannot play now!"

"Not until after dinner?" Alfreeda and I cried at the same time. "Come on, Mom!"

She didn't even answer us.

"And honestly, I can't take on Gracie today, Robert," Mom was almost shouting now. "I just can't handle another fighter around here! So quit trying to get out of your job. Doris expects *you* to dogsit on Saturdays when she's working, not me!"

Mom had started to wave her arms around

in the air, like a couple of battle flags in a fierce wind. Her face had turned sort of purple. The veins stuck out on her neck.

Man, it was real creepy, seeing my own mother like that.

Uncle Robert stepped forward. Now his nose actually touched Mom's.

I thought, *Uh-oh, here comes war.*

"Winifred?" he said.

"What?" she snapped and frowned at him.

"You," he said, "need a nap."

Suddenly Mom stopped frowning. She sighed and her stiff shoulders went loose.

"Actually," she said in a quiet voice, "there's nothing I need more right now."

"I know," he said and patted her shoulder.

"Let me guess. You're overworked. You didn't get enough sleep."

Mom nodded.

"Go," he said. "Sleep for a few hours. I'll take care of the hotel chores. The twins can play with Twinkles and the monster, I mean, Gracie."

"Really?" Mom asked.

"You bet," he said.

Man, I couldn't imagine ever doing something that nice for my sister. Not in a thousand years.

Then Uncle Robert hugged Mom. She hugged him back.

I thought, *That would never happen between Alfreeda and me. Not in a MILLION years!*

"Thank you, Robbie." Mom said. She dashed to the house.

The rest of us headed inside the kennel building. Gracie and Twinkles led the way. Uncle Robert held their leashes and walked in front of Alfreeda and me.

We didn't even make it through the office before she started to argue with me again.

All I'd said was, "Follow me, Twinkles. The Frisbees are in the storeroom."

Alfreeda yelled, "No way!"

Uncle Robert spun around and stopped. We bumped into him and shut right up.

He held up his hands. "Whoa," he said. "Seems like you kids are extra tired too. And let me guess. You're not getting enough playtime."

We nodded.

"We'll figure out how to fix that," he said. "But first, how about drawing straws to decide?"

"We don't have any straws," Alfreeda said.

"Okay then, pencils," Uncle Robert said and grabbed two off the desk. He grabbed them so fast, I didn't see how long they were. He held the ends in his fist. Our uncle has big hands, and all I could see were the dog-shaped erasers sticking out the top.

"Draw," he said. "Whoever gets the longest pencil gets to play with Twinkles first."

"No fair!" I cried. "She always wins! Even in a game of chance, she always beats me!"

Alfreeda grabbed a pencil before I even had a chance. She shrieked and cried, "Woo-hoo! I got the longest! It's not even sharpened!"

"See, Uncle Robert?" I frowned. "She always wins. At everything. Just because she was born five minutes before me, she always acts like she's the only alpha kid around our place! I can't stand it anymore!"

"Alfie," said Uncle Robert, patting my shoulder. "Slow down. Take a deep breath."

I did.

"Another," he said.

I did. Actually, the extra air made my head feel a little less like exploding.

"Now draw," he told me. So I did. I looked

at my pencil and laughed. "It's not sharpened either," I said.

"Right," said Uncle Robert. "It's a tie. You'll each get to play with Twinkles for thirty minutes. The other will play with Gracie for that half hour." He took off his watch and gave it to Alfreeda. "Take turns all day if you want."

"Hey!" I said. "How come she gets to wear your watch?"

"Because you, Alf, get to play Frisbee with Twinkles first," he said and handed Twinkles' leash to me.

"Cool!" I said.

"What?" Alfreeda cried. "Why him?"

"Because," Uncle Robert said in his same old laid-back voice, "you're the only one Gracie will listen to! You're top dog in her eyes. That's pretty cool, right?"

"Guess so." Alfreeda's frown turned to a grin. She took Gracie's leash. "Come, Gracie, let's go play catch." She led Gracie down the hall toward the play-yard door.

Man, I couldn't believe my uncle. He was blasting bad moods to pieces all over the place.

"Okay, bud," he said to me. "I'm taking the other dogs for a good long walk."

"All eleven of them?" I asked and laughed.

"Sure, why not?" Uncle Robert grinned and shrugged. "It's a big wide country road out there, Alf."

"Sure is," I said and grinned back at him. "Come on, Twink, old girl."

And she and I flew to the storeroom to get a Frisbee.

CHAPTER 4

Tug of Beak

Twinkles and I dashed from the storeroom to the play yard.

"Come on, Twink," I called. "Follow me."

Our grassy play yard is plenty big, so I led her far away from Gracie and Alfreeda. They were playing catch on the chicken-coop side of the play area.

Twinkles barked excited-like and ran beside me. She didn't take her big round eyeballs off the Frisbee in my hand. Not for one second.

Finally, I stopped and waved it in front of her nose. "Go get it!" I yelled.

I whipped the disk backhand. It flew across the yard. Twinkles shot toward it, then man, did she jump! She caught about two feet of air — and then she caught the disk!

"Wow!" I cried. "Way to go, Twink!"

She trotted up to me with the Frisbee in her mouth and dropped it right at my feet. She went, "Woof!" I knew exactly what she was saying: *Throw it again, Alf! Hurry up, slowpoke! Throw it higher!*

"You got it, pal," I said. "Catch this if you can."

I got a running start and whipped the disk as hard as I could. Twinkles tore after it and jumped even higher this time!

But she missed the disk. It got caught in the

wind and flew over her head. It soared toward the super-blue sky and sailed right over the fence.

It landed in the field grass on the other side.

Twinkles looked at me and barked.

"No problem," I said. "I'll go get it."

But Mom had the gate key on her key chain. She always kept the gate locked. So I climbed up the chain-link fence and sat on top of it, all set to jump.

Suddenly I froze. Two chickens darted over and started to fight for the Frisbee. For some weird reason, they both really wanted that toy. I'm telling you, it was like they were playing tug-of-beak!

Then Gracie shot to the fence. She stood right below me and started to bark her head off at the chickens.

Next, Spot flew over. He started to flap his wings and shriek at Gracie!

And what did Gracie do? She snarled at Spot and clawed at the fence, trying to get at him for a tasty rooster snack.

Man, I had to hang on tight. All the fighting made the fence wiggle like crazy!

Gracie stuck her nose right through a hole in the chain link, trying to get even closer to her prey. Spot didn't waste a second. His neck feathers puffed way out, getting ready for battle.

Then he pecked Gracie right on the nose.

Did Gracie back off? No!

"Gracie, come!" Alfreeda shouted. "Spot's really going to hurt you! Come!" My sister even stamped her foot.

But Gracie kept right on snarling and clawing and sticking her nose through holes in the fence. And Spot kept pecking at her nose. That had to hurt!

Super quick, Alfreeda leaped over and grabbed Gracie's leash. My sister tugged like a Saint Bernard hauling a hurt skier up a steep mountain.

She dragged Gracie about ten feet away from the fence. But then, Gracie dug her paws into the dirt and gave a good hard yank on the leash.

Alfreeda flew through the air like a human Frisbee. She soared for about five feet, then landed with a thud in a dirt patch. She kept hold of the leash through the whole thing! It was actually sort of impressive.

"Yow!" she cried.

Gracie dragged her for a couple more feet, and then Alfreeda wised up and let go of the leash.

I leaped off the fence and ran toward my groaning sister.

CHAPTER 5

Rooster Soup and Roasted Kid

At alpha-guy speed, I got the monster, I mean, Gracie, all shut up in pen number seven. Twinkles, too.

It wasn't easy though — it took all of my muscles to get those dogs inside.

Alfreeda hadn't helped one bit. She'd just dragged her feet into the kennel kitchen, real slow. Her knees didn't even bend. She walked real stiff-like and left me with the whole job. Figures.

I wiped my sweaty face with my sweaty Hound Hotel T-shirt. Then I stared through the chain-link gate at Gracie and shook my head. Uncle Robert had been right. Gracie was a fighting machine.

She paced back and forth, checking me out. I knew exactly what she was thinking: *Bring me rooster soup. Or maybe roasted kid. Don't care which, just bring MEAT!*

Twinkles lay on the little dog bed in pen seven. She panted hard.

"Hang on, Twink," I said. "I'll get you some water."

I went to the storeroom, grabbed a small water dish, and headed to the kitchen sink. Alfreeda was sitting at the table in the kitchen, trying to open the first-aid kit. She was using only her left hand.

I noticed the palm and fingers on her right hand were scratched up and sort of bloody. So were her knees.

Man, she was acting so helpless. She couldn't even get that box open with one hand. If you ask me, it shouldn't have been that hard. I almost laughed.

But I didn't. Instead, I remembered a time back when I was a little kid.

I'd fallen off a slide at some park in town and hurt my wrist pretty bad. It was so sore, I couldn't even put on socks by myself for about three days.

Alfreeda just kept trying to lift the latch with her left thumb and pointer finger. She grunted and pushed even harder.

Suddenly the box shot right off the table. It sailed through the air like a fat metal Frisbee and landed on the floor with a super-loud bang. The noise made her jump.

I didn't even laugh at that, which kind of surprised me. I just picked up the box and put it on the table. Then I opened it for her.

She took out a Band-Aid. She tore the wrapping off with her teeth. Then she tried to stick the Band-Aid on her right palm with her left hand.

Well, the sticky ends got all stuck to her fingers. She shook her hand, trying to get the Band-Aid off.

It came off, all right. It shot like a super-skinny Frisbee over the table and stuck to the wall. Alfreeda sighed and stared at her scratched-up hand.

I grabbed the box and dug through the first-aid stuff. I took out seven Band-Aids. I figured she'd need that many.

I opened them all and laid them sticky-side-up on the table.

Alfreeda stared at me.

"What?" I asked.

"Uh, thanks, Alfie," she said in a quiet voice.

"Whatever," I said and shrugged.

But for some totally weird reason — don't

ask me why — I didn't stop there. I grabbed one of the open Band-Aids.

"Hold out your hand," I said. I covered up some of the scratches. I put another one on her hand, then five on her knees. The right knee was more scratched up than the left. But they both looked pretty sore, if you ask me.

"Thanks, Alfie," she said. And that's all she said.

I just shrugged.

I filled Twinkles's water dish and headed back to pen seven. Gracie saw me coming and did a low slow growl.

"Back off," I ordered her. "This water is for Twinkles. I'll get you some in a minute, if you're nice."

I squeezed through the gate and set the dish in front of Twinkles. But right away, Gracie shoved Twinkles aside and drank all of the water herself.

"Hey!" I said. "That wasn't for you! Can't you see how thirsty Twinkles is?"

I frowned at Gracie and grabbed the dish. Then in my firmest army-command voice, I said, "Gracie, I'm going for more water, got it? For Twinkles. And you're *not* going to take one lick of it, you hear me?"

My voice had gotten pretty loud about then. I noticed that my arms had started to wave around like a couple of battle flags in a high wind. (If my face was purple or the veins stuck out on my neck, I don't know — I didn't have a mirror.)

I spun around and reached for the gate latch. Suddenly I heard a *whoosh* behind me.

I looked over my shoulder and saw Gracie

flying straight at me like a huge furry Frisbee.
But her mouth was wide open, and I saw a
bunch of pointy, sharp-looking teeth.

They locked right onto my rear end. "*Yow!*" I
yelled.

CHAPTER 6

This Is MY Territory, Dude

I screamed and jumped sideways. Somehow I yanked my rear end out of Gracie's teeth.

At alpha-guy speed, I scaled the chain-link fence. I dropped into pen eight and stood there for a minute, panting hard. And rubbing my rear too.

Okay, so it didn't really hurt. Actually, it didn't hurt at all. Gracie hadn't torn my jeans or anything.

But still. Maybe she could've drawn blood.

To be honest, I knew something cool about golden retrievers: they've got soft mouths. They can carry stuff around and not hurt it, not even small live animals.

Still, she had lots of big teeth. Maybe she'd given me a warning. Maybe next time, it would be bruises and blood puddles.

"Look, Gracie," I demanded. "You've got to let me into your pen, with zero attacks, okay? Twinkles. Needs. Water."

Gracie just eyeballed me. She sat right down in front of her little sister.

Well, I knew what she was doing. Not to brag, but I know a lot about dogs and wolves, how they operate in packs and stuff. My dad has taught me tons. It was easy to read Gracie's mind.

I was pretty sure she was thinking: *This pen*

*is MY territory, dude. I'm the leader of this pack.
And you're not a member of it. So get lost before I
bite your rear again.*

Fact is, I couldn't blame her. She was just
acting like her natural-born self. See, every
dog's great-great-great (add a bunch more
greats here) grandparents were wolves. Even
after so many great-great grandparents, dogs
are still part wolf. I mean, all dogs. Even little
pugs and big retrievers.

Dogs think their human families are their
packs. Every pack has a leader, and lots of
times it's not the human who's in charge. Real
often, the dog takes on the job of caring for the
whole pack.

So if a dog like Gracie decides that she's
the alpha wolf, then she has to become fierce.
It's her job to keep the weaker wolves safe by
fighting off enemies. In the wild, different wolf

packs are enemies. Wolf packs stay far away from each other. If another pack comes close, that usually means danger.

Well, standing there in pen eight, I figured it out: in Gracie's mind, she belonged to a pack with three members — Doris, Twinkles, and herself. In her mind, Uncle Robert belonged to some other pack. And so did I.

To Gracie, Uncle Robert and I smelled like danger. So she had to get tough with us.

I peered through the chain-link fence at her.

"Gracie?" I said. "You're one smart dog. But guess what? You better keep your eyeballs open. Because I'm about to outsmart you."

I marched out of pen eight and headed for the storeroom.

🐾 🐾 🐾

Pretty soon, I came marching back with a big Hound Hotel doggie pillow tied onto my rear end.

I'd wrapped a leash around my stomach about five times. I'd tied a double knot, too. That pillow was going nowhere.

I opened pen seven's gate and marched in.

"Hello there, Gracie Old Girl," I said in my coolest alpha-guy voice. I stepped right over her and grabbed Twinkles's water dish. Then I spun around, cool as a frozen doggie treat, and marched back to the pen door.

Suddenly I heard a *whoosh* behind me. I felt a hard yank on my pillow armor.

I looked back over my shoulder. Gracie had about half the pillow inside her mouth! I'm not kidding!

She started to growl and tug my pillow

armor from side to side. I got yanked back and forth, and she even spun me all the way around — twice!

On the third spin, I dived for the chain-link fence. Somehow I got a grip on it. With all of the alpha-guy power in my guns, I started to scale that fence.

It was no use. I made it up about two feet. Gracie had the strength of any female alpha wolf in the whole wide wilderness.

I hung on tight to the fence, even though Gracie kept tugging me left to right, right to left. It was getting harder to hang on. My fingers were killing me!

But I couldn't let go. Or Gracie would pull me to the floor. That's the last place anyone wants to be.

"Alfreeda!" I yelled. "Help!"

She came to the doorway and just stood there. She stared at me and wrinkled up her face. "You're weird, Alfie Wolfe," she said.

I hollered with all of my alpha-guy lung power, "Do something!"

CHAPTER 7

It's Your Fault, Alfie

Alfreeda sure took her time coming to my rescue. She moved real slow across the kennel room, her knees stiff-like. Maybe she was still sore from getting dragged by Gracie.

Finally, she headed into pen seven. She grabbed hold of Gracie's collar and pulled her away from me.

"Sit," Alfreeda commanded.

Gracie sat.

Alfreeda began to dig pillow guts out of Gracie's mouth. Then she went nose-to-nose with her.

"Listen, silly," she said. "We don't eat Hound Hotel pillows. We lay our sleepy heads down on them and have sweet dreams, okay?"

Gracie barked.

"Good," Alfreeda said to her. "Glad you understand. Now, stay."

Gracie stayed.

Alfreeda dug some dog treats out of her pocket. She laid them on the floor, and Gracie started to gobble them up.

Then slow and stiff-like, Alfreeda headed to the trash can on the other side of the kennel room. She tossed the pillow stuffing.

I was still hanging onto the chain-link fence.

My face was pressed against it. I didn't dare move an inch or a single muscle.

Alfreeda came back, then nice and slow, I put my feet onto the floor and turned around. I leaned on the fence and didn't move.

But right away, I realized I didn't have to worry anymore. Alfreeda had yawned and sprawled out on the pen floor. And Gracie had flopped beside her.

Alfreeda put her head on Gracie's stomach and closed her eyes. Gracie closed her eyes too. They both seemed tired of fighting and everything else.

Then Gracie started to breathe slow and deep. The fighting machine was out cold!

"Hey," I whispered. "How come she attacked me but not you? You're not part of her regular pack. I don't get it. It can't just be the treats."

"*Shh*," Alfreeda said. Her eyes were getting real droopy. I guess getting tossed through the air really wore her out. "It's your fault, Alfie. You must have forgotten — never turn your back on a dog that doesn't like you."

"I didn't," I said.

"Did too."

"Prove it," I demanded.

"The proof is in the pillow," she said and yawned. "You, Alf, for sure turned your back on Gracie. How else could she tear apart a pillow that was tied to your rear end?"

She had a point.

"Maybe you didn't notice," Alfreeda added in a sleepy whisper, "but I backed out of the pen when I went to the trash can just now. I backed out, smiling really wide at her, because —"

"Because," I interrupted her, "dogs are as afraid of our teeth as we are of theirs. And they're afraid of teeth and beaks on other animals, too. Yeah, yeah, I know."

"Exactly," Alfreeda whispered. Her eyes were almost closed now. "And that's why Gracie never bit Spot. Because Spot never turned his back on her. Dog attacks always happen from behind, because that's the side that doesn't have teeth. Or a beak . . ."

I almost shouted, *Stop telling me stuff I already know! I just forgot, okay? Give a guy a break!*

But I didn't. Because my sister's eyes were totally closed now. Besides, I'd figured something out, after watching Uncle Robert in action: keeping your cool when somebody tries to pick a fight is like dumping a load of ice on a fire. If you keep cool and act nice, the other guy will act less fierce.

Actually, alpha wolves are great at that. Sometimes, beta wolves pick fights with the leader. ("Beta" means "second," as in "second in command.") The alpha always keeps its cool and the beta backs off.

I looked over at Twinkles. There she was, still lying on the little dog bed. She looked thirsty and starved for Frisbee. I tiptoed over and whispered in her ear, "Hey, Twink. Let's go have some fun. But be real quiet, okay?"

She jumped up and bobbed her head. Together, we tiptoed toward the pen door.

Suddenly Alfreeda said, "Gracie, you're a totally bony pillow!"

I stopped and spun around. Alfreeda was wiggling around, trying to get comfortable on Gracie's ribs.

If my sister noticed that I was taking Twinkles out for some Frisbee, she would get up and try to take him away from me. Somehow, I had to get my sister to fall asleep and stay asleep. That was my only hope for extra time with Twinkles.

And I knew just what to do.

I whispered in Twink's ear, "*Shh*. Be super quiet, pal. I'll be right back."

CHAPTER 8

Frisbee Land!

I dashed to the storeroom and came right back. I had a bunch of Hound Hotel pillows and blankets in my arms.

I tiptoed into pen seven and whispered, "*Shh*," to Twinkles. Then I tapped Alfreeda on the shoulder.

She opened her eyes halfway and blinked real slow. "What?" she whispered.

"Here," I whispered back. "No more bony pillow. Take these."

I even helped her spread out the blankets and make a nice cozy bed.

"Uh, thanks, Alf," she said and looked at me, real surprised.

"No problem," I whispered and shrugged.

She put her head right down on a comfy doggie pillow. In seconds, she was out cold. She started to snore like a pug. Yes!

"Come on, Twink," I whispered. We tiptoed out of the pen.

Seconds later, we were in the play yard, with the door shut firm behind us.

"Here we are!" I cried. "Right smack in the middle of Frisbee Land! First, let's get you a some water, okay Twinkles?"

Quick, I got her a drink from the hose. Then I let out a whoop and grabbed the Frisbee.

With a flick of my wrist, the disk flew down the field.

"Go get it, girl!" I yelled.

Twinkles bolted across the play yard. She caught some serious air — and the Frisbee! She dashed back and dropped it at my feet. She barked like crazy. It was totally easy to read her mind: *Hurry up, Alf! Throw it again!*

So I did.

"Go get it, Twink!" I threw the Frisbee across the play yard again. Not too high. Not too far. Just right.

And nobody bugged us for a good long time. Way longer than thirty minutes!

It was the best cure for crabbiness in the whole wide world.

Is a Golden Retriever the Dog for You?

Hi! It's me, Alfreeda!

I HAVE to set one thing straight: many golden retrievers aren't a bit like Gracie! They're calm, friendly, and really gentle. So maybe you want your own beautiful golden now too, right? I don't blame you. Goldens make great pets for families! I mean, most families. But before you zoom off to buy or adopt one, here are some important facts you should know:

Goldens are large-size dogs that need lots of exercise. If you live in a little apartment, get a little dog instead. And if you can't promise to take your dog on a walk every day, don't get any dog. Get a goldfish.

Goldens shed. That means some of their hair falls out sometimes. Their waterproof topcoat sheds a little bit all year long. Their soft undercoat (which keeps them cool in the summer and warm in the winter), sheds in the spring and fall. If your family doesn't like dog hair on the couch or rugs, get a dog that doesn't shed, like a West Highland terrier.

Goldens are crepuscular. That means they're more active when the sun rises and the sun sets. They sleep more in the middle of the day. If people in your family like to sleep late, or don't like being bugged at bedtime, better not get a golden! (Because a tired family is a crabby family, right?)

Okay, signing off for now . . . until the next adventure at Hound Hotel!

Yours very factually,

Alfreeda Wolfe

Glossary

admit (ad-MIT)—to agree that something is true, often against your wishes

annoyed (uh-NOID)—to feel angry or impatient

bruises (BROOZE-ez)—dark marks you get on your skin when you fall or are hit by something

demanded (di-MAND-ed)—claimed something or asked for something firmly

guests (GESTS)—those staying in a hotel, a motel, or an inn

human (HYOO-muhn)—referring to a person

impressive (im-PRESS-iv)—having the power to impress to have an effect on someone's mind or feelings

interrupted (in-tuh-RUHP-ted)—started talking before someone else has finished talking

serious (SIHR-ee-uhss)—sincere and not joking

shrieked (SHREEKD)—cried out or scream in a shrill, piercing way

snarl (SNARL)—if an animal snarls, it shows its teeth and makes a growling sound

whistled (WISS-uhld)—made a high, shrill sound by blowing air through the lips

wilderness (WIL-dur-ness)—an area of wild land where no people live

Talk About It

1. Why do you think it is easier for siblings to get along when they are adults than when they are kids?

2. What important facts about working with dogs did Alfreeda remember that Alfie forgot?

3. On page 68, Alfreeda has shared some facts (and opinions) about golden retrievers. Do you think a golden retriever would be a good dog for your family? Why or why not?

Write About It

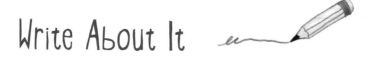

1. Since Hound Hotel has been so busy, maybe they should hire more help. Write a help-wanted ad, looking for a hired hand. Be sure to include the types of skills, experience, and attitude that are needed.

2. This story has many crabby characters. Write your own short story with at least one crabby character.

3. Research pugs and golden retrievers. Then make a list of three to five items that compare and contrast the two dogs.

Glossary

admit (ad-MIT)—to agree that something is true, often against your wishes

annoyed (uh-NOID)—to feel angry or impatient

bruises (BROOZE-ez)—dark marks you get on your skin when you fall or are hit by something

demanded (di-MAND-ed)—claimed something or asked for something firmly

guests (GESTS)—those staying in a hotel, a motel, or an inn

human (HYOO-muhn)—referring to a person

impressive (im-PRESS-iv)—having the power to impress to have an effect on someone's mind or feelings

interrupted (in-tuh-RUHP-ted)—started talking before someone else has finished talking

serious (SIHR-ee-uhss)—sincere and not joking

shrieked (SHREEKD)—cried out or scream in a shrill, piercing way

snarl (SNARL)—if an animal snarls, it shows its teeth and makes a growling sound

whistled (WISS-uhld)—made a high, shrill sound by blowing air through the lips

wilderness (WIL-dur-ness)—an area of wild land where no people live

Talk About It

1. Why do you think it is easier for siblings to get along when they are adults than when they are kids?

2. What important facts about working with dogs did Alfreeda remember that Alfie forgot?

3. On page 68, Alfreeda has shared some facts (and opinions) about golden retrievers. Do you think a golden retriever would be a good dog for your family? Why or why not?

Write About It

1. Since Hound Hotel has been so busy, maybe they should hire more help. Write a help-wanted ad, looking for a hired hand. Be sure to include the types of skills, experience, and attitude that are needed.

2. This story has many crabby characters. Write your own short story with at least one crabby character.

3. Research pugs and golden retrievers. Then make a list of three to five items that compare and contrast the two dogs.

About the Author

Shelley Swanson Sateren grew up with five pet dogs — a beagle, a terrier mix, a terrier-poodle mix, a Weimaraner, and a German shorthaired pointer. As an adult, she adopted a lively West Highland white terrier named Max. Besides having written many children's books, Shelley has worked as a children's book editor and in a children's bookstore. She lives in Saint Paul, Minnesota, with her husband, and has two grown sons.

About the Illustrator

Deborah Melmon has worked as an illustrator for over 25 years. After graduating from Academy of Art University in San Francisco, she started her career illustrating covers for the Palo Alto Weekly newspaper. Since then, she has produced artwork for over twenty children's books. Her artwork can also be found on giftwrap, greeting cards, and fabric. Deborah lives in Menlo Park, California and shares her studio with an energetic Airedale Terrier named Mack.

THE FUN DOESN'T STOP HERE!

Discover more at
www.capstonekids.com

VIDEOS & CONTESTS
GAMES & PUZZLES
FRIENDS & FAVORITES
AUTHORS & ILLUSTRATORS

Find cool websites and more books like this one at **www.facthound.com**

Just type in the Book ID: 9781479558995 and you're ready to go!